I0699098

KASEY FALLON

A TERROR TRIPTYCH

Ireland

Copyright © 2024 Author Kasey Fallon

All rights reserved.

979-8-9871956-5-9

*For Ireland.
One of the greatest countries
with the darkest histories.*

Contents

Legacy

We do it all for family:
Till the earth, and plant the seeds.

We do it all for history:
Mulch the beds and kill the weeds.

Everything we do
Is so that our line may live on.

Pushing forth the best of us
When the rest of us are gone.

We do it all for family;
Give offerings for blessings.

We do it all for progeny;
Even when the offering's distressing.

We do it all for family;
Careful now, or we'll do ye too.

Anything we do
Might happen to travelers passing through.

We do it all for family; our legacy; our history;
Come visit, for we've started giving tours
On our Fair Farm of Clairy.

Finn would be better than his father. He wanted to grow up to be like his father. Strong. Tall. His father knew *everything* there was to know about farming. So Finn would learn even more. Their farm was the best in the county; everyone said so, every season. And Finn wanted to make it even better. The Fair Farm of Clairy, they called it. They had the best land for planting and tilling. Had for generations.

As he carried another wooden crate of fresh vegetables across the north field, Finn watched his father assess the clouds rolling in. The weight of the crate dug into his fingers and strained his thin shoulders, but he refused to carry less. He had to do everything he could for the farm.

The young boy looked at the same clouds his Da watched. They would have rain before the end of the day. His Mam said he already had the sense of a farmer. He would grow up even *better* than his Da at reading the skies.

They would have rain by supper, Tiernan saw, with storms overnight. They would have to cover the younger shoots by then. He stood still, hands in his overalls, standing at the edge of their northern field between the plants and the trees. His gaze was stuck on the weathered fence separating the two.

Wind ruffled his neglected hair over his ears, the same black as his parents' before him, and theirs before them. Black Irish, they were called. The favored ones.

The Clairy Farm had stood for centuries, and thrived when others failed. He'd known the rumors, of course. The Clairys had made a deal with the Old Gods.

Just a story. Simple gab over fences and tea to explain the farm's success. Then as a boy, he'd felt the pull to the North Wood. He'd woken in the middle of the night, the air crystalline and calling to him.

Just beyond their farmlands to the north, a stone circle waited. If myth were taken as truth, as it often was anywhere in Ros Comain, the circle was left after faeries had used the area for magic. They would dance on Midsommar's Eve and the area would come alive with magics. And so the circle was called a danse. Even as a child, he had a healthy enough fear of the fae to never step into their danse.

The air had been charged with electric currents he couldn't see, but he imagined if he could, they would be brilliant blues and greens. Slashes of lilac and yellow would crackle through the air. He'd stepped beyond their land that night, just to the edge of the faerie ring. Waiting for him, crouched atop the highest stone, easily two metres in the air, perched a creature he hadn't seen since.

Tiernan had heard his voice over the years, he considered now as he raked his hand through his hair again. But he hadn't seen The Cromm since. It made a man feel mad, it did. But who would feel sane in an ancient bargain with a Gaelic God?

He'd woken in his own bed, the only evidence from the night in the mud and grass on his feet and pyjama pants. Tiernan kept trying to tell himself it was a dream. The encounter had haunted him to such distraction, he'd nearly raked over their ripe tomato plants.

His Da had sat him down, and explained their legacy to him then. Learning of human sacrifice at age ten had shattered his perfect illusion of the farm. Their family.

Murderers. Murder was their legacy.

He blew out a sigh as he turned his back on the North Wood and faced the stone danse stained in layered, black rivulets, long dried. It was here he'd learned that blood dries black. The site of so many horrific moments made saliva gather at the back of his mouth, ready to retch.

The sight of his son walking steadily through their rows of turnips soothed him. He turned his back on the North Wood, and decided to ignore the brisk dip in temperature. He forced his thoughts to other things.

The fields would be ready for harvest soon, and Tiernan knew he could count on the help of their neighbours when the time came. The favour would be returned come autumn, when the McAdams would need help lifting and cutting sod. Bogging work that, but it was part of a farmers' life. Comhair. Cooperation. Community.

Who would he kill this year? Would it be a McAdam? The thought turned his stomach, and he couldn't look at Finn any longer. The bargain weighed on him, more so every year; every year it came closer to telling Finn what it was they did. How they were so successful. How they'd survived the droughts, and famines, and still thrived.

The boy was only eight, Tiernan reasoned. He had a couple of years more to be a child. Maybe five, if they were lucky. With a determined stride he reset his farmers' cap on his head and went to fetch the fabric covering. 'Twould be a long night.

Thunder woke Finn. At least he thought it did. He sat upright in bed as fractured light shuddered across his bedroom. He was wide awake, though he'd been dreaming of the fields. He often did. Movement outside his window caught his attention. Finn felt his heart pound harder than the rain on the roof.

He crept to the windowsill, crouching low. The matching pyjamas his Mam got him for last Christmas brought out the blue of his eyes, she said, though he started outgrowing them in the spring. They resisted as he snuck forward. Pale blue fabric snagged over scabbed knees and he winced.

He kept his eyes squinted to peer through the curtains out into the rain. The farm was coal black, but there, just a few feet beyond his windowsill, Finn thought he saw someone walking away. A tall, thin man? Da! His Da had to be going out to cover the shoots they forgot, or maybe something had shifted in the storm. Finn pushed the heavy pane up and called after him.

"Da? Da!"

Finn heard nothing in return aside from wind and rain. He squinted, but the darkness had already absorbed his Da. He had to go help.

His feet skid on the bare floors as he sped to the back door. He hesitated only once, wondering if he should wake his Mam, but a howl of wind spurred him on as he

laced his boots tight. *Hurry,* it said. *To the North Wood.*
Finn didn't question the voice in his head. It was the
direction he saw his Da go. Not bothering with a raincoat,
he unlatched the back door and ran.

Drenched in seconds, Finn saw his Da's back
again, just for a moment through the downpour before he
lost sight of him. Finn put his hands to his mouth to shout
over the storm.

"Da!?" he called.

His father didn't turn. Finn ran into the north fields.
Every time he thought he was getting closer he saw the
tall, retreating form, he would call out, but his father never
slowed. By the time Finn reached the old circle of stones
on their border, his father was nowhere to be found. Finn
climbed a boulder to sit on top, shielding his eyes against
the rain.

"*DA!*" he cried. A light was on at the house, he saw.
For the first time, Finn realized it might not have been his
father he followed into the night.

"Finn Shannon Clairy," he heard from behind him.
"Youngest of the Clairys. Progeny of O'Clairgh, of Ros
Comain. Welcome to the North Wood."

The voice grated Finn's ears and soothed his fear
at the same time. The tone was gruff; the accent, heavy,
and he felt like he shouldn't have been able to hear it at all

through the rain. He pivoted atop the boulder, shifting and praying for balance.

Behind him, where there had been normal, simple trees, the rain now fell *around* them and the danse circle in sheets, creating a bubble. The trees seemed taller, and fireflies twirled in deep shadows. Finn pinched the inside of his own arm hard enough to bruise. He had to be dreaming. The voice spoke again.

"This is no delusion, boy. I am Cromm Cruaich, a God before you."

One shadow broke away from the others to stalk toward him. It reminded Finn of the scarecrow he helped his father build last year. Except this one was almost three metres tall, with full branches for arms that didn't stop moving.

Thin, spindly fingers moved restlessly. He wore a wide straw hat so deep in shadow he could only see the suggestion of a face, and where eyes should have been were empty black sockets. The fear came roaring back. Finn whimpered.

"Have no fear of me, young Finn. You and I are partners."

The Cromm Cruaich bowed low. A light thrumming sound filled the air, and the sound of it made Finn relax.

"Partners?" he asked.

"For the land, young Finn. Partners for the farm. We do it all—"

"We do it all for family: till the earth, and plant the seeds. We do it all for history: mulch the beds, and kill the weeds. Everything we do is so that our line may live on. Pushing forth the best of us, when the rest of us are gone," Finn parrotted. He was proud to have it memorised. His mother said it to him every night before bed.

The Cromm Cruaich seemed pleased.

"Very good. And do you know the rest of it?"

"Where else could he have gone?" Riona paced back and forth in front of the hearth. Water dripped off her curly auburn hair to reflect glimmers of light on the floor. "He's not out front, nae the laundry room, nae the attic, his window was open-"

Tiernan rubbed the back of his neck. He'd woken to the echo of his son screaming after him. Wind howled down the hall from Finn's open bedroom window, rattling every picture frame on the walls. Dread sat, a heavy knot in his stomach, weighing on his soul. The Cromm Cruaich had come for Finn, just as it had once come for him.

Riona knew about the legacy. He'd felt honor bound to tell her before they married. In truth, it seemed to bother

her less than him. But then she wasn't the one committing the… *offerings.* She never asked, and Tiernan never offered. And once every midsummer, just before the Lughnasadh festival, she cleaned the blood from his clothes without comment.

He cursed under his breath. They would be at the edge of the north fields. The centuries old ley line where The Cromm had made the first deal. His Gran had told him of other places, magical points where the Old Gods and Fae still walked, but he'd never sought them out. Why should he? One God was more than enough. He stood.

"The Cromm took him," he told Riona, unable to look her in the eye. The sickly knowledge of their son alone with the ancient being was constricting his chest. He hated this. All of it. Their entire life was built upon fields of blood. There had to be a way out. He strode out the front door, neglecting a jacket. He and Riona were already drenched from searching for Finn.

As soon as he stepped outside, the wind and rain picked up, pelting him in the face and pushing him back toward the house. The Cromm didn't want him interrupting, Tiernan realised with a sneer. Too fecking bad. This was *his* family. *His* land.

Finn frowned. There was more? He shook his head.

"We do it all for family; Give offerings for blessings. We do it all for progeny; Even when the offering's distressing." The Cromm paused. "Do ye know what that means, boy?"

Finn thought, scrunching his brow.

"We give people presents?"

"Very good, young Clairy. But not people. *Me*. Your ancestors made a pact with me. A deal was struck, on this very spot, almost two hundred years ago."

Finn looked around them in awe. He couldn't imagine two hundred years ago. Was the faerie circle here this whole time? Did it look the same? His Da said the farm hardly changed at all.

"Yer father has the right of it," the creature agreed.

Finn frowned, wondering if he said that out loud.

"There were a good bit more trees, but the land hasn't changed. The only thing that's changed, young Clairy, is the offerings."

His voice deepened, rumbling low enough that Finn felt it in his bones. Terror came rushing back, and Finn cowered low, closer to the boulder. A dulled scent reached his nose, coppery like blood, but musty like something left under his bed for a year. The shadows around them bounced wildly as lightning danced through swaying boughs. Rain beat harder, and their safe circle shrunk.

"Did yer parents teach you what Lughnasadh is?"
he asked.

Finn nodded, hunched low against the old stone.
"It's August? We have a festival."

The dark, imposing figure nodded. "Every
Lughnasadh, every harvest, every reaping of the land's
birth," he growled, "I would receive the best that Ireland
had to offer. Maids, babes, full grown men, the picture of
health. And now? Now I get elders; wise, maybe, but frail.
I get the sick. The infirm..."

The rumbling voice trailed off as he focused back
on Finn. He seemed to sigh, and the whirling shadows
eased back. The rain smoothed out to a steady mist.

"Do ye know what mouldy bread tastes like, young
Clairy?"

The Cromm turned his eyes to the fields. His jaw
moved up and down, as if he was chewing.

"It sticks to the roof of your mouth, and ye can taste
the rot as soon as you've bitten in. But if ye need the
sustenance; if ye need the food, then it's already too late.
Ye can't spit it out. You just have to chew, the fuzzy,
spindly dregs sticking between your teeth. Swallowing is
worse, and it sits claggy in your throat. Then your gut
clenches and tries to get it back out, but if ye don't have
any other food, then ye have to bear it."

The sockets where eyes should have been looked at Finn's place on the weathered rock again. Nausea roiled below Finn's ribs and his heart raced.

"*You* wouldn't give me mouldy food, would ye, young Clairy? The Cromm Cruaich?"

Finn shook his head frantically. The Cromm Cruaich smiled. It should have been a kindly gesture, but a thin trail of sweat trickled down Finn's spine. Maybe it was just the dark edge of the woods casting shadows, he thought, but inside the smile were no teeth. Just gaping blackness.

"Finn!" he heard from the field.

The rain picked up again.

"Da!" he called back, twisting atop the short wall. Rain hit him full in the face and he nearly fell.

"Finn Cillian Clairy! Get offa the danse! What were you thinking, coming out here in a storm? To these woods?!"

His father was walking odd, slow and hunched forward, as if it were a struggle to get across the field. Finn wondered if he'd hurt himself. Finn jumped down from the stone.

"Da! Are ye hurt? I was—"

"Finn, ye cannot be out here!" Tiernan yelled as he approached.

"*See?*" Finn heard in his ear. He turned, but the trees beyond him were empty. The Cromm's voice continued, smooth and quiet on the wind. *"He doesn't respect me. Doesn't respect the bargain. Doesn't respect you."*

Finn scrunched up his face. That couldn't be true. The Cromm Cruaich was a *God.* He did good things for their family. For their farm. That was *everything.*

"But," he started to answer, and was cut off as his father approached.

"We'll speak soon, young Clairy." And the voice was gone.

Finn ran to his father.

"Da! Did ye see! It was one of the Old Gods—the Cromm Cruaich, he said, and—"

Tiernan reached him and dropped to his knees. The grip he took on Finn's arms had him pulling back in pain, but Tiernan didn't let go.

"Da—"

"I don't care what he's said to ye, boy." He shook Finn in a way he never had before. "Ye cannot do as he says. We are good people, Finn. We don't have to keep a deal made hundreds of years ago. We won't."

He rose, pulling Finn behind him. Tiernan screamed out at the forest.

"Do ye hear that?! There will be no more deal! The Clairys are *good* people! We won't be taking people's lives!"

His Da broke off into a sob and turned to hug Finn. Barely able to breathe while wrapped in his father's arms, Finn couldn't keep up.

First the gods were good, and everyone said their farm was the best, and everything they did was for the farm, and now his Da was crying because the God was bad and their farm wasn't going to be the best? Who was taking lives? Didn't they do everything for the farm?

"Da, I think he's just… hungry, maybe?" Finn said, hesitant. He spoke quietly as the wind and rain died down.

Tiernan sniffled and looked at Finn with red eyes.

"He said what now?"

"He was just talking about gifts, and how he didn't want any moldy bread anymore," Finn said. "And Lughnasadh, he said the deal was for offers on Lughnasadh."

"Offerings," Tiernan corrected absently. His eyes narrowed on Finn.

"Did he say what the offerings *are*, Finn?"

Finn thought hard. *Had* the Cromm specifically said what the presents were? There was the talk of old people… a whisper drifted over his shoulder.

"Nothing that isn't already mine, young Clairy. And all of Ireland is mine."

Finn looked up at his Da.

"He said nothing that isn't already his."

Tiernan stooped low and picked Finn up, like he hadn't done in a good long while. Finn patted his back as they made their way across the fields.

"Finn! Tiernan, ye've brought him back," Riona said as soon as they walked through the door. She dropped to her knees to wrap Finn in a hug. Tiernan scrubbed his hands through his hair.

"Auch, cul an tir, what am I thinkin of, we're making a mess in the house," he said.

Mud was everywhere. The rainwater sluicing off them forced swirls of dirt around the floor.

Tiernan ushered Riona and Finn to bed. He took both of their muddied clothes to soak overnight. He hoped his wife and son hadn't seen, but mud and rainwater weren't the only things they'd trekked in.

Blood swirled with blades of grass as he pushed the mop back and forth. Amidst the wet slop before he wrung it out, Tiernan heard a scrape; a knife against wood. He paused and lifted the mop. A dark puddle of brown and red sat in a divot just inside the door.

Their farmhouse was old and worn, and though it had withstood generations, it showed its age here and there. The floors were the original hardwood, and Tiernan winced at the thought of damaging them with an errant stick. He knelt.

Most of the mess was cleared, save for this puddle. As he stared, confused, the boards lifted from the floor and began to separate. Two boards stopped an inch and a half, each piece crooked and bent. They should have broken, he thought, staring at the warped wood. He spied lumps poking through the foamy, bloodied mud. They pushed up as if by invisible fingers.

Grimacing, he pushed his fingers into the divot, collecting chunks until there were no more. Tiernan stood and looked in his hand. Still wet, glinting in the lamplight, shone individual human teeth.

"I killed every one of these people—*my* people—meself. Ye think this will make me do what ye want, Cromm?" he whispered.

"Just a reminder, old friend," drifted from the window across the room. "This farm is built on the blood of *your* offerings."

Tiernan clenched his hand tight enough around the teeth they bit into his skin.

"Don't you humans have a saying?" the Cromm asked, his tone amused. "Something about sleeping in the bed you make." The voice turned into a hiss in Tiernan's mind. *This is the bed the Clairys have wrought. Generations of blood.*

Tiernan's own blood dripped from his fist to swirl with the blood on the floor. Blood, he saw, that was rapidly receding back into the earth through the floor.

"The Clairys are good people," Tiernan said, jaw locked tight.

The boards in front of him melded together again until they sat just where they had before. He heard the angry hiss again.

Good people uphold their bargains.

Tiernan knew without responding that the Cromm had gone. The cloying pressure in the air dissipated. The breeze felt fresh instead of suffocating. The rain persisted throughout the night and Tiernan watched every gale, rolling decaying teeth in his hand.

The next morning, Tiernan stumbled from bed. He'd overslept because he'd been up all night, seeing if the Cromm Cruaich would come back. But the only company he had was rain and a handful of loose teeth. Teeth that were currently rattling around in his nightstand drawer, as he didn't know where else to put them that Finn couldn't find.

Eyes squinted and gritty, Tiernan pushed his hands through his hair. God, he needed tea. He stubbed his toe on the doorframe and was too busy rubbing his foot in the hall to notice the voices at first. Finn's voice saying his name caught his attention.

"But Da said—"

"I know what yer Da said, Finn. But I just want you to think about it. Everything we do…"

"—is for the farm," Finn finished.

Tiernan couldn't believe it. Riona was *encouraging* their son to keep the deal? To kill people? It couldn't be. He opened his mouth and was about to turn the corner when Riona spoke again. He hesitated.

"Your Da is a good man, and he cares about us, and the farm, and you most of all, Finn."

Tiernan felt a rush of warmth for his wife. She understood him.

"I just don't know if he's strong enough to keep a deal with a God," she said, and his rush of affection burst.

"I could be," Finn said.

Tiernan backed away, gripping his head in his hands. It couldn't be. They couldn't. This wasn't happening. Blindly, he walked to the back door. Heedless of being barefoot or last night's rain, Tiernan slammed the door open and ran outside.

"Tiernan?" he heard behind him. He didn't look back.

Running past the shed, the glint of metal caught his eye. He changed direction, not slowing, kicking up dirt from rows of young shoots. They would likely die. For the first time in his life, he didn't care. He would end this deal once and for all.

The pickaxe was heavy, with a bit of rust where wood met metal, but he grabbed it without stopping and sprinted towards the North Wood. He realised his goal as soon as the old fence came into view; his body had moved faster than his mind. There would *be* no *offerings*, he thought furiously. With no place to *put* them, or *accept* them, the Cromm couldn't *have* them.

And the Cromm would have *nothing*, Tiernan decided as he swung the pickaxe overhead, from *his* family. From *their* farm. The first blow glanced off, shooting sparks into the air.

The second hit carved a chip the size of his hand out of the top of the monolith. It took several more swings to make a crack, but a farmer's life and the furious drive to protect his son gave Tiernan strength.

Young Clairy, you must hurry, Finn heard from the open back door.

"Hurry where?" he asked aloud, and his Mam turned from the sink to look at him oddly.

The North Wood, said the Cromm on the wind. *Your Da is hurting me. Hurting the farm. He's trying to break the pact. You must help me save the farm.*

Finn looked up from his bowl of oatmeal - the butter had just melted all the way, and the raisins his Mam had put in hadn't gotten soggy yet - it was perfect. The back door his father had run through minutes ago stood open.

"But what do I do?" he asked.

Help me save the farm, it repeated, more insistent. Finn jumped as a gale blew through the house. His Mam said nothing, but righted cups as they rattled and tipped. *Hurry, young Clairy!*

"Mam, the Cromm said—"

"I don't need to know what he said to you, Finn," she said kindly. She knelt in front of him. "If the Gods want me to know, they'll tell me. This is for you." She brushed a lock of hair away from his face. "I'm sorry, Finn Shannon. You're too young for this. But this is the way of it. I'll help you if I can, but you listen to the Cromm Cruaich."

Finn nodded and jumped off his chair. He paused long enough to jump into his boots before running into the field. The wind was there at his back, urging him along. No, Finn realized, it was *pushing* him along, helping him run faster. He reached the North Wood in only minutes.

His Da was there, furiously hacking away at the stones with the pickaxe. Was this why the Cromm was worried? Finn wondered. About the circle of faerie rocks? Maybe the Cromm was afraid of angering the faeries too?

"Da!" he called.

Tiernan turned, and Finn was shocked to see tears streaming down his father's face. Both froze for a long moment, looking at each other.

"Go home, son," Tiernan said. He turned away.

"Da, The Cromm Cruaich said—"

"*Do not listen!*" his father roared with another swing at another boulder. It cracked and a split ran down a third of it. "Do not listen to a word that creature has to say, Finn Shannon Clairy, and you *go. Back. To. The House!*" Each word was punctuated by a swing of the pickaxe.

Finn watched, his mouth open. What was he supposed to do? But there was something strange happening to the stones. Each time he blinked, his father had made another chip or crack; half of them were repaired before his Da had got to the next stone. Was the Cromm *fixing* the big rocks? Did he want the stones that bad?

Yes, young Clairy. We need the fae danse. It's part of the deal. Without it, your farm will die. Everything will die.

"Da! The farm will die!" Finn called.

"It will *not!*" Tiernan screamed. He turned away from the circle. "We have been farmers for generations. We *are* the farm, Finn, and we do not need the Cromm. We have *our* land, we have *each other,* and we have *Comhair!*"

His Da turned back, and let out a frustrated scream at the repairs to the ancient stones. He threw the pickaxe to the ground and started pulling at the small rocks with his hands. He pried up two from the ground before Finn heard the voice again.

Hit him with the axe, young Clairy. You tried. Nothing else will stop him now. You must save the farm.

Horrified, Finn took a step back.

"I can't!" he squeaked. He couldn't *kill* his Da. Not even for the Cromm.

Hit him with the blunt side, it said. *It will only stun him, so I can repair the danse. It won't hurt him.*

Finn hesitated, swallowing back tears. Maybe it would be okay, if he only stunned him a bit, he thought. He took small steps to the axe, looking down at it.

Young Clairy, do it now, or the farm will be lost! the Cromm cried.

Finn picked it up. It was almost as tall as he was, so he had to hold it close to the head. His Da had taught him that; the top part of any axe was the head. He would hit his Da's head with the back of the axe, he decided, and the Cromm could fix the stone circle, and his Da would just have a headache, and they would save the farm.

He pushed the heavy axe up above him, blunt side forward.

Amused, it watched the boy approach the man hesitantly. The attempted ruination of his sacred site initially had him outraged, but this was well worth it.

He saw the determination on each Clairy's face. And laughed. They would all lose, no matter how determined they were.

As the axe fell, with a single thought from the Cromm, the air around the axe spun. It twisted in the boy's hands.

The wet *thunk* of the pickaxe going into Tiernan Clairy's skull was a sound he would cherish forever. Horror dawned on the elder and young Clairy's faces as they realised what happened. The Cromm felt the hot blood as soon as it reached the ground, free-flowing out of the father's head. The euphoria was heady and instant.

Already on his knees, Tiernan didn't have far to pitch forward until he rested, ironically, on one of the lower stones. The rush of energy the Cromm felt was immediate. It was a thirst too long ignored, and he drank greedily.

Refreshed, he watched with curiosity what the young Clairy would do. He had yet to do anything but stare at his father's body. The Cromm frowned. He knew humans could be fragile. If he had mentally broken the youngest Clairy—

Riona crested the rise on her way to the North Wood, and the Cromm considered her. She was not a blood relative, but she would have made him a good partner. He looked at the ground in disgust. Better than her husband had been. He wondered what she would do.

She took in the scene briefly, and turned around. The Cromm was curious enough to follow her. He remained unseen on the wind as he drifted after her to the shed.

He'd learned that humans took a rather critical and horrified approach to his physical form. And then they made parodies of it with men made of straw, he thought acerbically. Idiotic beasts, all of them. But without them, and their offerings, his strength waned. The Cromm hated that he needed them.

Riona reappeared wearing a heavy leather apron and carrying a wickedly curved sickle. Oh, she wouldn't, he mused, fascinated. Would she?

She approached the stock-still Finn and her husband's body with tears streaming down her face. Both living Clairys remained silent, so the Cromm did as well.

After one fast slice, the younger Clairy - the only real Clairy, now, he thought - pivoted on the grass to vomit. Finn retched until he heaved only air.

The scent of the filth bothered the Cromm, so he sent the wind in the other direction. It took another two swings before the elder Clairy was fully beheaded. The Cromm silently applauded the woman. She would have made a fine partner indeed.

"Finn," she said, her voice thin. She tried again. "Finn. You have to place the offering."

The boy looked up at his mother, horrified. Riona kept her gaze to the ground.

"It has to be you, Finn. He's already gone. I'm sorry."

She jerked her head to the farthest boulder.

"There, I think. Just... set him—" she faltered, "*it, set it* there, and we can go home."

The Cromm watched the boy stand and take shuffling steps towards his parents. He had never had parents, he mused, but it seemed difficult.

The young Clairy's eyes flit everywhere but the scene in front of him as he approached the severed head. What was left of the man's tongue and throat fell from the father's head as the son picked it up off the ground. A steaming string of Tiernan's throat lining landed with a wet splat in the grass as his tongue lapped at air out of where his neck used to be.

"Da—" he said weakly.

"Tis not your Da," Riona said. "Your Da ran off with a tourist. He's in England now, I think."

"England?" Finn asked, his voice brittle.

"That's what we're going to tell anyone who asks. Go set that thing on that stone there, Finn, that tall one, and we can go home. You saved the farm."

"I saved the farm?" he repeated, and the Cromm wondered again if the boy were mentally damaged.

"That's right. Now go on."

As Finn walked to the far end of the Cromm's stone danse, Tiernan's seeping, frozen face turned away, Riona picked up the feet of her dead husband. With all her body weight she leaned forward, dragging him around the boulder. As entertaining as it was to see her struggle with such a mundane task, the Cromm was appreciative of his new partners. He was feeling generous.

With a thought towards the earth, it began to shift, bringing Riona and the body past the edge of the trees with no effort. Riona gasped, startled into dropping Tiernan's legs. She stepped back, and the Cromm felt gracious enough to sink the body into the ground for her. Within moments it was out of sight, and he even bloomed a couple of flowers over it.

She sniffled. The Cromm frowned. Didn't humans appreciate flowers?

"Thank you," she whispered, and he was appeased.

"Mam," Finn said. The boy stood just beyond the fence, eyes wide and glassy, staring at the ground.

Riona wiped the tears from her face and stepped forward to wrap an arm around her son. The Cromm went to fetch his meal, satisfaction and power singing through his veins, when he heard them in chorus.

"We do it all for family. Till the earth, and plant the seeds. We do it all for history. Mulch the beds and kill the weeds—"

His laughter mingled with the wind across the stone danse, and across the fields of green.

The Dead House

On the Isle of Inis Oirr
Awaits a house,
Desolate and austere

Sea salt seeps in every crevice
While inside
Sleeps a most curious menace

For no soul's ever seen it
Or no soul that's made it back
For once ye're in, ye're in for good,
Inside the house of grey and black.

So avoid the Dead House of Aran,
On the Isle of Inis Oirr,
Or ye'll never leave the house that's barren.
The children might remember the fear,
But we'll move on like ye never happened.

In a chiming echo, reminiscing a happier life, bells ring across the island town. It doesn't matter which bells; school bells; church bells; the clanging of fishing boats in and out all day, or the melancholy expulsion of a fog horn.

The heartbeat of the island-town Inis Oirr pulses with every chime heard through town. When to wake. When to go to school. When to go home. When you pray. When you die. The bells let school out at three, but Clara won't get home until well after four.

After the bells toll, telling them school is out, she decides to take the long way home. Except it's not really a conscious decision, so much as her feet walking her away from school and down the opposite hill. Her backpack thuds and sways with each uneven step down the dirt hill. She passes the turnoff for the Plassey Wreck. She knows it's one of the biggest things to ever happen to their island. It's what brings most of the tourists in, her Da says, but it's never held real appeal for her.

Past the rusting corpse of the Plassey is the oldest cemetery on any of the islands: Cnoc Raithní. She loves taking walks there. Passing through the ornate stone archway makes her feel like she's entered another world.

An older one. She knows there are the bones of a saint buried somewhere, and the cemetery dates back to 1500 BC, but her focus is always on the sinking remnants of the church.

While the roof caved in long ago, Clara loves the winding path leading her down into the ground. What steps are left are narrow, and she has to duck beneath the stones of one of the two remaining doorways.

Sitting in what used to be the pulpit, she stares up at the faded faces of angels. Grand wings, once white, still reach for the heavens up the damp, salt-crusted walls. She wonders how they survived all this time, when so many other things don't last at all. Her thoughts circle back to the Dead House.

It's on her way home from Cnoc Raithní, and she climbs her way out of the cemetery, her footsteps light and eager. Her eyes already fixed ahead, she strides farther down the wide beaten path, to stare. To wonder. To get… just a little bit closer. Every day, for months now. Some days a foot, others an inch.

There's something pulling at her about this lonely, broken place. The worn old house draws her gaze; her attention; her thoughts; even her dreams. But even in her dreams she's never made it inside. When she's awake, there's something inside of her that wants to go in.

It's the only house on the island that hasn't been painted in ages. Like her, the house isn't done up in the same bright colors as everyone else. Gutters droop low or dangle broken off, discarded by the roof and weather.

Today, she's crept around the edge of the stone wall that borders the front yard. Just one toe around the corner where crumbling stone meets the sandy grass. The yard has been dead for years. This *place* has been dead ever since she can remember, but no one will tell her why. *The family moved on long ago*, her Da said. In between knits, her mother told her not to worry about it and *won't she be a good lass and hand her that other set of needles?*

She remembers a boy who lived there with his Gran. At least she's pretty sure she does. His father was a fisherman, she recalls, stepping just a stone closer to the house. They couldn't have moved on *long ago* if *she* remembered, right? She was only eleven. Did she play with him? Egan, maybe? She struggles to remember as she gazes at the house.

The vines strangling one corner of the house look different from the ones in her Ma's garden. These are darker, and so thick they cast their own shadows. The strands reach around the front as fog off the water envelops it from behind.

It stands apart from the rows of the other houses across the island. Tilting her head, Clara thinks it looks like nature is choking the house. Or maybe giving it a hug. She'd never seen a house need a hug more.

It sits only metres in front of the crashing waves, but up a small rise. Like her, it sticks out from everything pretty around it. She can't tell what color it used to be, but it's varying shades of grey now, lighter tones on top. Every window is shuttered, or, where the shutters have broken off, boarded with various fragments of wood.

Clara stares intently where there are gaps in the wood and through the windows still intact. Even though nothing moves, inside or out, she feels like something is looking back at her. The house *wants* her to come in. She hates that the house looks sad. It just needs someone to mow the lawn, she thinks, and leans forward without realizing.

"Go on in then, if you love it so much!" came a voice from behind her.

Startling, Clara jumps back, hitting her knee on the low stone wall. She turns to face the main road of Inis Oiir; a hard-packed dirt path, stones and shells poking through.

"Clara loves the Dead House, Clara loves the Dead House," they chant.

The small cluster of girls stand on the far side of the path. Their outfits are nearly identical, as are the sneers they send across the road. With her homemade sweaters (even though her mother *is* one of the best knitters on the island) Clara has never fit in. She prefers black to pastel; reading to boys. The teasing never stops. Even though her parents tell her every time to be the bigger person, Clara can't help but get drawn in.

"I don't love it!" she called back. She ignores the stinging in her knee to hurry back to the road. Twin drops of blood fall from her knee to the weed-choked ground. They're absorbed as soon as they fall. The ground tremors, but Clara is focused on the girls.

"I just want to see—"

But the girls are already giggling down the street without a backward glance. She stares after them, clearly remembering them making fun of Egan the same way. She *did* remember him. Why didn't her parents? Looking longingly at the grey house, Clara steps off the grass, not noticing the overgrown blades bending towards her.

"We are a community as one," Ms. Hurley says. Her eyes dare any of her fifteen pupils to look away. None do. "Storms come in, or if there's a lack of fish, or Saints forbid a boat goes down, who do we have?"

"Each other," the children say in unison.

Ms. Hurley nods in satisfaction.

"If ye see somethin' strange, or a neighbor in need, you go see if they need help!" She thwacks her meter ruler against her desk, sending sheets of paper flying.

Two students jump from their seats to catch them, and Ms. Hurley smiles.

"Well done, lads. All of ye, remember what I've said, finish yer lessons at home, and we'll go over them on Monday."

After twenty years of teaching, Ms. Hurley has the rhythm of Inis Oirr perfected, and the school bell rings just as she finishes speaking.

Clara dawdles, putting her things away. Maybe, she thinks as she latches her bag, maybe Ms. Hurley knows more about the abandoned house. She dreamt of it again last night - but it had been glowing from the inside, and beautiful on the outside. She'd woken up excited to see it, peering out her window in hopes of seeing the old house lit up down the hill. Only the dark night and crash of waves greeted her instead.

The shadows beckoned her outside, but she'd hesitated. Clara approaches Ms. Hurley now, wishing she'd gone to see the house last night.

"Ms. Hurley?"

Her favorite teacher pauses as she wipes down the blackboard.

"Aye, Clara?" she asks, her voice gentling. Ms. Hurley has always been kind to her, and even spoken with parents about how some of the students treat her.

"I-I was wondering if ye knew anytin' aboot the grey house, down by the cemetery?"

Ms. Hurley turns back to the board so quickly that her silvershot bun of hair whips sideways.

"Nothing much, child. Ye ought steer clear of it. It's very old."

Clara looks at the floor. She shifts her backpack and digs the point of her shoe into the wood floor. Ms. Hurley finishes erasing the board, but still doesn't turn around. Her voice is quiet.

"I had a brother, Clara. He used to like that house too." She turns and crouches so they're eye to eye. "Ye mustn't go into the house."

A fine thrill snakes up Clara's spine. Ms. Hurley knows more than she's saying.

Clara stands on the hill above the Dead House. Pebbles and fragments of shells poke into her bare feet. She takes one step forward, then another, the breeze catching her soft blue nightgown. Although she doesn't remember falling asleep, the voices waking her up were clear as the bells that run island life. She must have heard the voices from down the road.

The Dead House spills light out across the lawn. Every overgrown patch looks better somehow, bathed in flickering light. Her steps grow surer the closer she gets. Voices and music flow out of every window.

Maybe someone's moved in, she wonders. Or maybe the little boy and his family have moved back? Something rustles in the bushes underneath the window to her right, and Clara pauses. Would someone be mad at her for coming over? It sounds like a ceili. Clara had always wanted to go to one of the big parties. The grownups would talk about them for weeks.

A small rabbit pokes its head out from under a spindly shrub. It doesn't move, just stares at her, with big black eyes and twitching whiskers. Clara comes a step closer. Still it doesn't move.

The grey rabbit plants one paw forward. In the off-yellow light from the window, his nose beats a frantic rhythm against the shadows. Clara glances at the window, creeping closer, but no one is at the glass.

Her neighbors had rabbits once. They kept them in a wood hutch out back. Maybe this one is like those? She reaches out a hand, and she's delighted the rabbit stays still. He bows his head, allowing her to pet the velvety soft fur at its neck. Maybe the grey house is magic, she thinks. It must be. Where parties happen at night and rabbits let you pet them.

She's so intent on the rabbit that she's startled by the sudden silence. She freezes. They stopped the music. Did someone see her?

With her heart in her throat, Clara crouches low beneath the window sill, one hand still on the rabbit. She's terrified to look, but her eyes are drawn up. Up over the faded ledge of the window. To the panes of glass where shadows have stopped moving inside.

No one is there. After another minute of silence - where has everyone gone? she thinks - she looks back to the rabbit. She should go home. Maybe she could take him home, too.

The rabbit still has his head down, but he's breathing heavy now, his ribs expanding wide and rapid beneath her palm. She watches a line of saliva fall from his mouth. Frowning, she starts to draw her hand back. He might be sick.

He snaps his head up to meet her eyes. The black eyes are rimmed in red now, and as she watches, his teeth grow longer, sharpening into jagged points. Clara falls backward, unable to breathe. The creature tenses, its back legs coiled to spring. It leaps.

Clara sits up, gasping. Her covers are on the floor in a heap; her sheets are twisted, pinning her to the bed. She yanks her hair out of her face, wincing at the tug on her scalp.

She's never had a nightmare like that before. Already the details are fading, but she remembers the Dead House, and the party… her brow furrows as she tries to recall. There was something else. Something scary?

But she's never been afraid of the Dead House.

The curtains at her window flutter. There's a chill in the air coming off the water, and it seeps into her. Wrapping her blanket tighter around her shoulders, Clara creeps to the window. She could wake up Mam and Da, she thinks, but they'll just tell her to go back to bed.

Stars have taken over the sky. As her gaze slides over the cemetery and the large hill hiding the Plassey Wreck, a light winks on down the path. *The Dead House.*

Eyes wide, Clara stops breathing. It's just like her dream. She feels the pull, right from her heart down the path to the Dead House. It beats in time with her heartbeat. In concert, the low horn of a boat drifts to her from the water. She *has* to go see. Maybe there's a party, like in her dream!

Clara drops the blanket where she stands, pulling a matching knit sweater over her pale blue nightgown. She's walking through the living room when Ms. Hurley's warning surfaces through the steady thrum of her need to run down the hill to the Dead House. Next to the hearth, she stops. Frowns.

There was something about the dream… something scary? She can't remember.

Her mother's basket of knitting needles reflects in her periphery, and Clara takes one. It's from a smaller set; thin blue ones, and fits perfectly in her hand. There. Now if anything scares her, she can scare it back.

From the top of the hill, Clara remembers her dream more clearly. It's happening right in front of her all over again. Her bare feet take hesitant steps over the shells and hard earth.

The same wind she felt from her bedroom window blows more insistently, whipping her hair around her head. She can just barely hear the music from the house on it. A layer of gooseflesh runs down her arms, and Clara wraps her arms around herself, the knitting needle poking her in the side.

Golden light pours from every window. It lights up the overgrown yard, just like in her dream. The grey walls look black in the night. Clara hesitates at the edge of the yard, one hand on the stone fence, her eyes on the bushes in front of the house.

As something moves behind the low branches, Clara's grip tightens on the needle. Before she can make another move, the front door of the Dead House opens wide, spilling light and music out to her.

The music makes Clara smile, the darkness of the night and her knitting needle forgotten, falling from her hand. She walks up the weed-filled path, the blades of grass caressing her feet in welcome. Two steps into the house, the door swings closed silently behind her.

Ms. Hurley's hands tighten on her book bag as she approaches the Faherty's front porch. Her hands want to tremble, so she squeezes tighter.

Clara's mother is out on the front porch, rocking and knitting, face tilted towards the sun. A piece of Ms.

Hurley's worry loosens. Clara must have simply come down with something, she assures herself. Her absence from school had nothing to do with the Dead House.

She remembers being only eight when her brother disappeared. He'd had a similar obsession with the Dead House. Dreamt about it even. It had bothered her, but nothing compared to the fear of waking up to his empty bed.

The terror and the confusion. No one believed her. She'd thought she was going mad. Everyone acted as if he'd never existed. They'd called Ryan her 'imaginary friend'. She'd never seen him again.

"Mrs. Faherty!" she calls from the path, one hand in the air.

Without missing a beat of her knit, Clara's mother smiles in absent greeting.

"'Mornin'. It's Ms. Hurley, isn't it?"

Ms. Hurley steps up to the edge of the porch.

"It is, yes. I've brought your daughter's assignments since she's missed the last two days."

Mrs. Faherty clacks away with her knitting needles. She idly wonders where her other blue needle is. She smiles at the woman.

"Sorry, dear. Ye must be confused. I've never had a daughter.

Dungeons Under Dublin

The fires couldn't burn us
And the torture made us mad
Ensnaring you in here with us
Is the most craic we've ever had

We were tried for treason
Whipped and pitched with tar
And when they couldnae find a reason
Turned us into what we are

Across the centuries we've gathered
Growing stronger, darker, madder
And in the centuries that come
Our prison will stand all the prouder

For we're the residents of Dungeon Dublin
Underground forever more
And we may keep you here with us
Finally evenin' the score

For all the scores that stood against us-
The Scots, the Norms, the Dutch and more
The Celts will win out in the end
Erin go Bragh is what we kill for.

The burning across his scalp was miserable tonight. Paddy scrubbed his fingers viciously over one ear, muttering a curse when his fingers came away wet. He often scratched till he bled, but it was worse recently. He blamed the damp of the dungeons for his condition. Every so often a decent breeze would waft in from somewhere, but it never cooled his scalp. Never enough.

He woulda' been to a physician, but he didn't trust 'em. Not after his Mary, God bless her soul. She and their son were lost to him in the birth bed, but he prayed every night for them. Physicians couldn't do a damned thing to help. Wouldn't, were more like it in his mind.

With a tired sigh he fit his cap gingerly back on his head and returned to his rounds in the tunnels. His tunnels were in the older part of the underground. Not the *oldest*, as they were still trying to fortify those enough to be rebuilt after a hundred years of disuse, but he figured they'd get to it. Maybe after he was gone.

After almost fifty years working in the dungeons, he felt every ache and creak in his bones. His jaw ached something fierce.

A set of footsteps approaching caught his attention, and he frowned. Hardly anyone came through his part of the tunnels. He could go weeks without seeing a soul on his shifts.

Well. His eyes skittered the shadowed parts of the tunnel where his lamplight didn't reach. Maybe he'd seen a soul or two, but no one living.

"Who's there?" he called into the dark beyond his light.

The footsteps stopped.

"Hello?"

"Ayah," Paddy said, and turned a corner. "I said who's there?"

He stopped short to stare at a young man, fresh-shaven, buttons on his uniform still shiny. Paddy sighed. They hadn't told him a new lad was starting tonight, but then again, they never did.

"New guard, son?"

"Yes! Yes, sir. I'm sorry, I didn't realize, that is, they didn't mention anyone else was working in this section."

Paddy laughed. The rough sound bounced off the stone and wood, down tunnels long enough the echo would be heard long after he stopped.   "They never do.

Didn't tell me a new guy was startin' either." He held out his hand. "Paddy Donnelly, son."

The young man's grip was stronger than his voice. "James Walsh Smith."

Paddy narrowed his eyes. A burst of anger split through his chest, there and gone before he could grab it.

"Walsh? Any relation to Dr. Angus Walsh?"

James - Jimmy, he decided to call him - leaned back at Paddy's tone.

"Noah, no sir, not any that I know of."

Paddy relaxed again. He smiled at the younger man.

"That's alright, then. Ye're skinny, Jimmy, but you'll do." Paddy gestured the way with his light.

They spent every night together for a fortnight with Jimmy telling jokes, Paddy's bark of a laugh echoing off the old stone, while Paddy coached him on the tunnels. Jimmy shared pictures of his girlfriend, and Paddy shared stories about growing up a poor farmer's son with mischevious siblings, all six of them.

"D'ye put any stock in the rumors, Paddy?" Jimmy asked one night. He handed Paddy an apple. Paddy knew where the conversation was headed. He sighed as he bit into the apple, his jaw twinging in pain. He rubbed it absently, not surprised when it creaked under his hand, shifting unnaturally. It had been doing that as long as he could remember.

"Which ones, Jimmy? The prisoners of war we keep down here, or the politicians with their secret meetings?"

The younger man looked around furtively. As if there were anyone to overhear, Paddy thought.

"The *rumors*, Paddy. About what else is down here. What might not be…" Jimmy gulped. "Human, maybe."

The two men eyed each other, so different in age and so many other ways, Paddy thought, but somehow they'd become friends. Jimmy continued.

"Ye *know,* Paddy, I know ye do. The ghosts and what-all down here. Folk say the souls cannae rest while we still use the dungeons. Even if it *is* just for politicians and what-all."

Paddy stroked his chin and fought the urge to scratch at his scalp.

"Aye, lad. I know what people say."

Jimmy stared up at him, eyes wide.

"Well?" he asked when Paddy said nothing more.

"Well, young James, I can tell ye I've seen things. Can't tell ye what they are, or were, but I can assure ye we're not alone down here."

He kept walking and softened his voice. Didn't want the spirits being offended they were gossiping.

"Spirits what been through too much. Too hurt here to move on. Mebbe waitin' on a bit of revenge, I'd wager."

Jimmy's voice was a whisper. "On us?"

"Hard to say. Could be the people they need revenge on are passed, so they'll be waiting forever." His footsteps slowed until they both paused at a split in the tunnels. "Or, could be they're just waiting."

"Waiting on what?"

Paddy shrugged one shoulder. Jimmy sighed and looked down the tunnel beyond their circle of soft yellow light.

"I don't know if I believe in it all, Paddy. Me Gran does, and she was the first to tell me to not take this job. But if they exist… if they're here… I hope I don't meet 'em."

Paddy wrapped his arm around Jimmy's shoulders.

"No need ta worry, Jimmy. If somethin' unnatural comes, I've got ye, boy-o."

Paddy lost track of time, as it was easy to do in the tunnels. Jimmy joked about getting even more pale and looking like a ghost. One evening, before they'd even started their rounds, the radio Jimmy wore crackled to life. Paddy refused to wear his.

"*All* crew, please meet at tunnel forty-tree fer a meetin'. I repeat, *all crew.*"

Meaning him as well, Paddy thought, sighing, and wondered if that had been repeated just for him. It wouldn't be the first meeting that he'd skipped out on.

"Where's tunnel forty-three?" Jimmy asked him, and Paddy realized that Jimmy pronounced his *-th-*" like an Englishman.

"Where did ye say ye're from, Jimmy?"

"County Claire, but I went to school in Wales for a while. Plenty of people ask me about my accent," he said.

Paddy stared at him long enough Jimmy flushed pink, even in the lamplight.

"Your family's got ta be well off ta send ye to school all the way over in Wales then, eh? What on earth are ye doin' workin down here?" Paddy asked.

Jimmy scrunched his brow and tilted his head.

"It was-"

His radio screeched.

"West Gate tunnel, report to forty-tree!"

Paddy gestured.

"Atta way, boy-o."

They hurried, but Paddy's mind stayed on Jimmy's schooling. From Galway to Dublin were far enough, but to travel *out of Ireland* for school? Must be well connected as well, he figured, to have no trouble for an Irishman there and make it back in one piece. Something wriggled at the back of his mind, but he couldn't dig it out. Something he ought to remember. He let it go as they approached a group huddled around sawhorse tables and maps.

"They're gonna start here," their supervisor said as both men nestled into the fold. He nodded, acknowledging he'd seen them. Geoff, a tall, muscular man who looked more fit to *dig* the tunnels than to run their guards, Paddy thought, but never said so.

"Are the rest of the tunnels safe?" a man piped up from the back. A murmur went through the group.

"They're doubling the reinforcements around all three adjoining tunnels before they open anything," Geoff said, hands in the air in a gesture of calm. "The only change in rotation is going to be to the West Gate tunnels."

Geoff nodded at Jimmy. Next to him, Paddy nodded back. He would look out for the lad. He seemed a decent boy, even if he *had* spent time in England.

"The new"—Geoff's face scrunched—"*old* tunnels will be part of yer new rotation."

Paddy frowned. Why were they going into the old tunnels?

Jimmy piped up, and Paddy was glad he didn't have to.

"I know I'm new here, but is it normal then, to open up the older tunnels? Do we do that a lot?"

Geoff stroked his deep red beard. He was quiet long enough that the crew started shifting and Jimmy ducked his head, afraid he'd spoken out of turn.

"Not normal, Jimmy, no. Those tunnels haven't been open in a long time. But with—" Geoff hesitated. "Needs must is all, gentlemen. We're needing a bit more space is all I was told. So they're opening 'em up."

A few more questions were bandied before Paddy and Jimmy returned to their side of the tunnels.

"Tomorrow," Jimmy marveled. "No one's been there in maybe a century, Paddy, think of it! And we get to see it *tomorrow!*"

Rage, unbridled and unbidden, swept through Paddy.

"It weren't a *century*, ye nitwit," he snarled. His face pinched tight in a scowl.

Jimmy reared back from their shared circle of light. Paddy blinked, and the anger was gone. He felt the lines of his face smooth back out.

"Boy, I'm sorry, I, ah—doesn't feel all that long ago, is all. And tis not a pretty history for us. I had family here."

Lost in thought, he stepped past the boy. He said nothing more and preceded Jimmy down the tunnel. It was nearly an hour before Jimmy approached him again.

"Paddy, I didn't mean ta—I didn't know, I mean I know it was awful, I just—"

"It's alright, lad," Paddy cut him off. He raised him lamplight higher in an effort to lift the mood along with it. "But I'd wager that whatever their reasonin' is, they should leave it be. All they're goin' ta find is more ghosts."

Their next shift came with an eager tension in the air. Everyone went about their business as usual, but Paddy noticed the curious and worried glances cast, mostly at Jimmy.

"Come on lad," he said, an arm around him, "it's just another day in the tunnels."

Paddy noticed the smell first. The scent of upturned earth should have been fresh, thought the farmer's son. Instead, fetid air greeted them on their first round. They would finish their normal rounds first, Paddy decided, *then* go to the old tunnels. Jimmy was unusually quiet as they heard the occasional shout or machine echo.

"Ye alright, boy?" he asked.

"Fine, fine," Jimmy said, though his downturned face said otherwise. "My Gran called yesterday. Said she had a vision and to not come to work."

"Ye told her about the old tunnels?" Paddy asked, surprised.

"That's the thing," Jimmy said, shaking his head slowly. "I didn't."

Paddy frowned.

"Make way!" came from ahead of them. The heavy smell of wet cement coated Paddy's throat and irritated his scalp. The work crew had set up more lighting here, and he pulled his cap down over his head. He winced at the pain.

"Security!" he called ahead of them. Jimmy chimed in, and together they made their way through newly positioned beams and stripes of wet stone up the walls.

"They really meant reinforcement," Jimmy whispered.

Paddy shook his head in agreement. The walls looked almost brand-new, and each entry was being fitted with steel brackets at every corner. He made eye contact with Jimmy just before they were waved through the main gate to the old tunnel. Paddy grimaced at the rusted gate, thinking again they should have left it locked.

Fewer men worked on this side of the gate, which Paddy was fine with. He was so used to the dark and quiet that the blinding spotlights and sounds rebounding off every wall seemingly forever were giving him a headache. Someone swung the gate closed behind them. The harsh metallic clang echoed through his brain, even more than the echoes.

That *thing* - the insidious worm at the back of his mind - was wriggling again. Paddy could feel it. It tried to dig its way out, and his eyes burned. He squeezed them shut. It tried to climb up and his scalp felt on fire.

"Paddy?" Jimmy called from down the hall.

Paddy blinked and realized he hadn't walked much beyond the gate. The crew was opening and closing it, over and over. They added oil and new screws here and there. He stood, staring at where the gate clanged against stone.

"Paddy?" he heard Jimmy say again. "Don't we need to walk the whole perimeter?"

"Ayah, Jimmy, I'm comin'," he said, and hurried away from the awful noise. It resounded through his skull even as they walked away.

"Doesn't seem like they found anythin'," Jimmy said. His voice was quiet, almost reverent.

A prickle at the back of Paddy's neck had him looking over his shoulder constantly. Just because they hadn't found anything, he thought, didn't mean nothing hadn't found them.

"We shouldn't be here," he murmured. "No one should be here."

They heard a voice ahead of them and paused, looking at each other.

"Was anyone else down here?" Jimmy asked, eyes wide.

"Not supposed to be," Paddy said. "But remember, they don't always tell us everything."

The squirming thing inside his skull was writhing, twisting. It sent spears of pain through his skull, adding to the furious pulsing of his scalp. Unable to take it any longer, he tore his cap from his head, sighing as the air hit it.

"What do you think—" Jimmy stopped as he looked at Paddy. "Christ Almighty, Paddy, your scalp—it's bleeding!"

"Ayah," he said, turning his cap over to inspect the inside. It was covered in blood and little white flakes of skin, like it was almost every night. Patches of old blood had dried and turned black, thick and stiff as he grazed his callused fingers over it. "It's a condition."

"Do ye want to go see the medic? He's got to be on hand for all the work—"

"Don't trust 'em lad. Never trust a doctor. Don't see 'em for my jaw, my scalp, or anytin' else." He nodded towards the split ahead of them. "We should check out the noise, yeah?"

As they made the turn towards the right, he grabbed a small piece of chalk out of his back pocket, marking the way. If they got lost, someone would know where they went, or they could find their way back.

He walked ahead, leaving his cap off. Now that the boy had seen, he figured there was no need to have it on all the time. He'd never been ashamed of it. It was just a part of him, like his teeth or his heart. There was a small part of him that was almost proud of it, though he couldn't say why.

They continued in silence. Jimmy's breathing came a bit faster the deeper they went. They came upon rows of empty cells, most with the doors canted and falling. Heaps of fabric scraps sat on the floor. The dark tunnels seemed endless, as did the scraping inside Paddy's mind.

"Do ye think we should keep going?" Jimmy asked.

Silent, Paddy kept walking. He turned the bloody cap in his hands over and over. They stopped at another split and without hesitating Paddy turned left. Chills clawed their way from his burning scalp down both arms.

"Paddy, ye didn't mark the turn. Paddy?"

Jimmy grabbed for his arm, but Paddy couldn't feel it. There was something ahead. Somewhere he had to get to. Even the squirming tension in his brain stilled as he got closer. Like it wanted to go there too.

Almost there.

Jimmy followed silently. He heard scraping in the dirt; Jimmy marking the path his own way. Good lad. The burning - the creeping dread - the chills - the itch - all intensified as they stepped onto stone.

"This part of the tunnels, young Jimmy," Paddy said, his voice almost a sing-song, "this was part of the original castle. The floors, the walls, everyting is stone." He paused. "It's why it didn't burn."

Paddy felt drips of blood coming past his temples and down over his collar. He didn't wipe them away. An echo of a voice drifted to them from the far tunnel. Paddy didn't even look; it felt like an old friend. He felt no fear.

Jimmy puffed shallow breaths out his mouth.

"The quarter right above us was where they did it, James. They tried us. Tortured us. They executed us. Hundreds. Tousands. People would come and watch."

"Who, Paddy?"

"The English, lad. The English."

Paddy could say no more as he turned one last corner. A cell stood before them, no more remarkable than the others, but Paddy knew this was it. He gently toed open the iron door. Like in many of the others, a small pile of nothings sat in a heap in a corner.

A tin plate, he saw as he got closer, for feeding the prisoners. *If* they were fed. Grey remnants of fabric. The fierce need to push the fabric aside left him no choice.

A thin slice of white grinned up at him, teeth still attached. With trembling fingers he picked it up. The bottom half of a jaw, he realized.

The worm inside his skull had friends, he felt. And they were all trying to get out at once. He clutched his head and dropped to his knees, letting out a keening wail.

"Paddy! Please, let me take ye to a doctor—"

Paddy let out a low scoff. "No doctor can help me, boy. *Look! Look at what they did to me!*" he screamed, thrusting the jaw bone at him.

Jimmy went paler than the bone he held, the freckles across his nose standing out in dark contrast.

"I was one of the last," he whispered. "They'd already killed most of us. They found me hiding in me cousin's barn outside of Swigo."

Jimmy was shaking his head no as he crept back from Paddy. He tried to speak. No words came out. Paddy stayed crumpled on the ancient stone floor, rocking, his bleeding head in his hands.

He remembered now. The worms in his head, wriggling, screaming for air, they'd exploded into horrifying scene after scene of memory. The fear of hiding. The terror of being found. The manacles about his wrists and neck. The worst… he groaned with the memory. He could only be grateful that his Mary had passed before then.

The crowds, the onlookers, *picnicking* while his friends and family were executed. The stone below him was stained with black rivers. He knew the buckets of blood it must have taken to make all those stains he was dragged over. The blood of his people. The bonfire illuminated the grey-cast day in his mind's eye, as well as the bubbling pail of tar. He didn't have any answers. Knew nothing beyond where his own friends still hid, and still they tortured him. He never uttered their names.

"They pitch-capped me, lad. They poured steaming hot tar over me head, and scalped me with it." His breathing came ragged. "And when they got sicka' my screamin, they hit me so hard with a bat, my jaw damn near came off."

His eyes were drawn to it now, resting in Jimmy's hands. His skin felt too tight. His scalp felt afire once more. His hands clawed at air. All the hatred - the injustice - the pain - the torment - the grief - the forgotten - the remembered - all barrelled out of him in an inhuman howl as his body disintegrated.

Wind swirled in, carrying Paddy's screams all around them. The man in front of him wasn't a man. A spirit. A demon. Jimmy couldn't make sense out of what was right in front of him. Even the jawbone he held didn't seem real.

The man he'd spent months getting to know - getting to *like*, wasn't even alive. Half-alive? Jimmy didn't know.

Paddy fell still, half-crouched to the floor. His eyes remained locked on the piece of jaw that Jimmy held. The screaming had stopped only a moment ago, but it still echoed through the tunnels. Jimmy's mind and ears rang from the deafening tones.

As Jimmy watched, Paddy's skin shrank tighter. His cheekbones pushed through the thinning skin, and the sockets of his eyes turned black. In seconds, his skin turned to slate leather. Every cuticle tore free of his fingers, splitting to reveal long, narrow nails.

Paddy's fingers clawed at air, and Jimmy stumbled back, unable to draw a full breath. Where the skin at his scalp had been patchy and bloody, strips of skin now hung freely, pouring blood onto the stone floor between them.

The skin around his mouth drew up, up - tearing free where his back molars poked through. His lower jaw was no longer, his tongue dangling in midair as if tasting it. The piece of bone in Jimmy's hand was suddenly slick. He looked down to see it covered in blood and rough patches of skin.

"Paddy—" Jimmy whispered.

What was once Paddy took a step toward him on protruding knees. His worn out jumper made sense to

Jimmy now. Paddy had never been a guard. He was a prisoner.

Eye sockets still fixed to his own mandible, he held out a hand, shrunken and withered.

Jimmy felt the wetness of the jawbone's saliva against his hand. He levered it up, trying not to stare at Paddy's tongue flapping out of his neck.

The spectre wrenched the jawbone out of Jimmy's hand and turned away. Jimmy inched back in the cell. An awful slurping and cracking echoed in the small chamber. Jimmy had backed almost to the door when the sounds stopped. The near-skeleton whirled and surveyed him, boots to cap. His jaw was attached.

With a mirthless chuckle, he knelt to the floor, the jumpsuit bagging and poking at odd angles. He picked up the cap "Paddy" had dropped and righted it on his head. When he opened his mouth, a thousand voices spilled out.

"The fires couldn't burn us, and the torture made us mad. Ensnaring you in here with us is the most craic we've ever had."

Jimmy turned and ran, his boots slapping the stone. Laughter rang out behind him, a thousand different pitches and tones. At a fork, he saw his own scratch marks in the dirt and pivoted right. Whispering echoes accompanied his labored breathing.

"We were tried for treason."

Jimmy lost his footing, turning his ankle. He ran through the pain.

"*Whipped and pitched with tar.*"

Remembering how Paddy's scalp looked heightened the nausea in Jimmy's gut.

"*And when they couldnae find a reason, they turned us into what we are.*"

What? He thought frantically. What in God's name were they? The collection of spirits, then? Every person wrongfully tried in Dublin? For *centuries?* He should have listened to his Gran. He heard footsteps behind him. Terror blinded every thought beyond escape as he followed Paddy's markings.

The opening to the old tunnels beckoned. The workers had moved beyond it now, into the cells. Wide eyes looked on as Jimmy's arms pumped and he leapt over materials. He debated stopping to close the iron gate, but couldn't leave the workers locked in with that thing.

Jimmy screamed as he passed through the gateway. "*Run!*"

The responses faded even as the words followed him.

"Whoa, mate—"

"Seent a ghost, he did—"

"Oy, piss off, he's just spooked—"

The blood in his veins felt like ice as he realized the work crew was English. The voices came roaring through the tunnel. Jimmy didn't stop.

"Across the centuries we've gathered, growing stronger, darker, madder. And in the centuries that come, our prison will stand all the prouder."

Screams replaced the chanting rhyme. Crunching, shattering bones and pleas for mercy echoed after him. Tears streamed down Jimmy's face as he sprinted through the corridors. He passed a small cluster of guards smoking. A new rhyme filled the air.

"We're the residents of Dungeon Dublin, underground forever more. And we may keep you here with us, finally evenin' the score—"

"Fer feck's sake," he panted. "Run!" He plowed straight past them.

The light around him grew steadily until he realized he was almost out of the tunnels. No noises followed him. He could have wept. His footsteps stuttered to a shuffling jog. Thoughts rioted from place to place, hitting everything like a streak of lightning; the crew, those awful cells, the sounds that echoed, Paddy's jaw, all the *voices* coming from that… *thing*, and under it all, the terror of looking death in the eye.

A cold wind blasted from behind him, shoving him to his knees. Jimmy glanced over his shoulder. Just behind him, Paddy's skeleton brought the shadows with him. They swirled in riot around him as he held out a clawed hand towards Jimmy.

Paddy's eyes were gone now, lost to gaping sockets. Blood still flowed from his scalp as he looked down at Jimmy. Leathery tendons snapped as he moved his jaw and the voices spilled out.

"For all the scores that stood against us—the Scots, the Norms, the Dutch and more, the Celts will win out in the end."

It drew closer, and Jimmy closed his eyes. He couldn't watch death come for him. After a moment, the echo of voices stilled. Sweat beaded his upper lip and streamed down his temples. He opened his eyes.

"Paddy?" he whispered, hesitant.

For a moment, Paddy's eyes looked out at him from the cavernous face. Paddy's voice was *just* louder than all the others.

"Ye're skinny, Jimmy, but ye'll do."

With what might have been a wink, the bony figure stepped back. The whisper called out to Jimmy from the darkness.

"We're the residents of Dungeon Dublin, underground forever more. The Celts will win out in the end. Erin go Bragh is what we kill for."

EMERALD TRINITY TIMES

DUNGEON DOOM

The Garda are asking for Ireland's help.

Eighteen men and nine women vanished last week in the tunnels under Dublin castle. One man reportedly escaped, but has been unavailable for questioning. The Garda requests that anyone with information on the whereabouts of James Walsh Smith reach out.

Photos from Kasey's trip through Ireland

The perfect mug I wish I'd brought home

Moonlit walk outside Saint Patrick's Cathedral, est. 1191

Inis Oirr Graveyard, est. 10th century

The loch at Dunguaire Castle

Dawn at Saint Mary's Claddagh Church; Galway, est. 1891

Galway Cathedral at the River Corrib

Made some friends

Nag's Head on the Cliffs of Moher

About the Author

    Kasey grew up along the East Coast, from Maine to North Carolina. She is a multi-genre author becoming known for her gripping psychological works. With degrees in Criminology and Sociology, Fallon is interested by all aspects of social psychology, and is becoming recognized for her unique ability to blend psychological depth with emotional poignancy. Her characters are chillingly relatable, both dead and alive.

    She and her dog can be found investigating hiking trails, or curled up together on the couch as he nudges her computer off her lap to make room for himself.

Visit Kasey Fallon Online

**Visit the Author Fallon website!
Get Kasey's free monthly newsletter, _The Foreword,_ for new releases, book recommendations and more!**

Instagram:
@writ_fallon

Facebook:
Kasey Fallon

**Kasey is on Goodreads: Leave a Review!
Every review means so much.**

Cover Design by Margo Hawthorne

Margo Hawthorne is an alias for an author that likes to dabble in all things creative, including cover design. She spends her time writing, reading, painting, playing piano, and collecting rescue pets.

You can learn more and see her designs at margohawthorne.com.

Also by Kasey Fallon

Tai wasn't sure he could make it. With the sun in his eyes, he licked his lips and tasted only salt. His heart pounded and although he was half submerged in water, he could feel the sweat pouring off him.

He inhaled deep, twisted his hips and kicked his legs just in time to catch the barrel of the wave. He knew the instant his feet caught on the board and its layers of wax, and he felt the world drop away.

This. This is what it was to fly, he thought, directing the board with nature and physics. Water; salt; air; wax; gravity; wind; all rolled together as he soared towards the coast, until he dropped from the board to drift in.

The bright yellow of the board was a perfect foil for the aquamarine waters off small Rumi Island. He heard his friends cheering him on from the beach. With a huge grin, he waved and figured that was his best wave of the day, and a good place to stop. Instead of soft sand, sharp shells and pebbles met his feet as he walked through the shallows. Wincing as he felt another small cut, he figured maybe this was why this beach - although great for waves - was almost empty.

"Tai!" Sonya rushed into the low waves and jumped up for a quick kiss. "That was awesome. How was it?"

"Great. I mean it's not the same as using your own board, and it's been a long time, but man that was cool. Where's Rob?" he asked, looking around.

"He said he had to get back to the marina, but he said you could bring the board back whenever."

"Yo Tai! I forgot you even surfed?!" James, one of his best friends all through college, shambled up to the water's edge, beer in hand.

"Haven't in like five years man, but I grew up surfing. California all the way." With a grin, he wrapped an arm around Sonya's shoulders and carried the borrowed surfboard under the other arm. The other couple of their group, Shannon and Mariyah, were sitting with their shoes and towels. Sitting wasn't really accurate, he thought with an inner smile; they were just making out. They'd been together about as long as he and Sonya, but he thought they might last longer. They just seemed so... in tune.

As they approached the girls separated, but kept holding hands as they peered up. "You guys think we can head out soon?" asked Shannon, "I know I used sunscreen, but I'm still starting to burn." Sonya smirked a superior grin, and said

"Sorry chica. You guys want to quit the beach for Shannon?" she asked, looking at the group.

Tai frowned; she'd made it sound like they had to leave because of Shannon, but they had all been ready to leave anyway. He said as much, and got a relieved little smile from Shannon while Sonya stepped away from him.

"Man, I'm starved. Didn't Rob say there's a little shop right around here?" James asked, looking around the empty beach. They all looked around; while there had been a handful of people around earlier, the beach was now empty. Tai remembered that there weren't even any lifeguard stands, or flags to tell people what the riptides were, and it had been weirdly difficult to access. They'd had to walk over a half mile and then climb through and over rugged boulders between dense stands of trees to even get to the trail that led to the beach.

As he looked across the sand and into the trees in the silence, Tai heard whispers.

"What is that?" he asked, head cocking to the side. It seemed to come from all over, but when he closed his eyes to listen, it was coming from the trees.

"Rob told me the locals think this place is haunted," Sonya stated, rolling her eyes. "I mean obviously nobody comes here because of these freaking rocks."

"Don't you hear it?" Shannon said, eyes wide.

"I mean I hear something, but there's obviously nobody here." Sonya said with a hair flip. The group remained still for a minute, listening.

"I heard of this place, up in Maine, on the east coast? Where if you're quiet at these cliffs, they echo off the rocks and it sounds like thunder or clapping." James said.

Tai looked at him as James finished his beer. It could be something like that. "Yeah," he said nodding, "maybe there's a cave or something nearby that just echoes."

"Well Rob told us that that store has a little deli, with sandwiches and stuff?" said Shannon, standing to slap the sand off her bare legs. "He said it's through the trees to the right, but that we shouldn't go off the boardwalk. He said people get lost around here every year."

"Because people are stupid," Sonya said with another hair flip, adjusting her barely-there bikini top. Tai thought the breakup might be coming sooner rather than later.

As the group gathered their towels and made their way up the beach, Tai hung back, staring at the waves and listening to the whispers. It might be haunted, he figured, but it was still beautiful. Up the beach, the path took them back to the craggy boulders, where the trees pressed in from both sides. Tai thought it strange that he heard no birds, although the whispering was still faintly there. He heard the laughter from his friends ahead, and the swaying of branches, and nothing more. Instead of the salty ocean air, here under the canopy the air smelled stagnant, like layers of decay. Must be the leaves, he thought.

The trees shot straight up with a soft grey bark, and no low branches. Their slender boughs seemed to sway in tandem as he peered up. Haunted or not, he thought, it was definitely melancholy. Staring up, Tai didn't notice the fog that wound towards him, creeping with grasping tendrils.

Sonya shook his shoulder roughly. "Tai!" What's wrong with you?"

He jolted, and dropped the surfboard that had sat loosely in his grip.

"What?" he asked.

"What are you looking at? I've been calling you for like ten minutes. I turned around and you were just gone."

He shook his head and picked the surfboard back up, switching arms. "Sorry, I guess I just zoned out. Surfing must have worn me out more than I thought." With a grin, he shook his head and blinked a few times. They continued up the path and reached the fork where the group waited on the wooden planks.

"You okay man?" asked James.

"Yeah, just spaced out for a minute. I must be beat. I need food!" With a high-five to James, he picked his way over the last of the larger rocks, surfboard in tow.

"Do you want to just leave that thing here?" asked Sonya. "You can just put it behind some rocks or something."

"I don't mind," said Tai, "I don't want anything to happen to it. Boards are expensive."

"There's nobody even here, it'll be fine," Sonya argued.

"Sonya, enough. It's not mine." he said, and started walking. The rest of the group fell in, awkwardly silent.

"So what kind of food do we think some rando deli-shop on a remote island even has?" James asked the group. Everyone chuckled, except Sonya, Tai noticed, but the tension eased.

"Ooh, I hope they have tropical smoothies," Shannon said, happily swinging her hand in Mariyah's. Tai looked over at Sonya, who was staring sullenly into the trees as they walked.

"What about tropical tacos?" James said. The girls laughed, and Tai joined in until he realized Sonya had fallen behind them. With a little sigh he held back and waited until she caught up.

"What's wrong?"

"Nothing," she pouted, staring into the canopy. She pulled back when he went to take her hand and they stopped on the narrow path.

"You never hold my hand anymore." she said.

"I just tried to!"

"Yeah, only when something's wrong. And you took Shannon's side on the beach back there, and then you totally spaced out while I was talking to you - it's like you don't even care about me anymore."

"What sides?" he asked, "All I said was we were all ready to leave." Dragging a hand through his hair, he scented the salt from the waves, and wished he were back in the water. The trees were towering, making him feel claustrophobic. He'd felt the rift between him and Sonya, but he didn't want to have an argument. "Can we not do this now? We're standing on a little island, in the middle of the Bahamas. A literal paradise with our friends."

"*Your* friends," she mumbled, looking away from him.

"What does that even mean?" he asked, stepping back from her.

"It means I'm always alone!" she shouted, and slapped her hand over her mouth, shocked at what had slipped out. She backed away from him, eyes wide, before turning and sprinting into the trees.

"Sonya!" Tai shouted, looking up to the path to where their friends had disappeared around a curve. Remembering Rob's warning about people getting lost, he started into the trees. He saw a shadow of her black hair ahead and ran a little faster. Minutes later, he stopped to listen. At first he heard nothing, and saw little through the trees - and the low fog that had come in. "Sonya?" he asked, although his voice sounded dim and muted, even to his own ears. All around him the trees looked the same; tall, where he couldn't even see the tops of them, and eerily similar. No wonder people got lost here, he thought uneasily.

He gazed up, looking into the canopy. Whispers crashed in to fill the silence, and the surfboard slipped from his fingers, forgotten. Like the roaring of a wave, it was everywhere. Thousands of low voices, murmuring; whispering; he couldn't differentiate any voices, or words. Not at first. He closed his eyes, struggling to hear - maybe one of the voices was Sonya's.

Don't be afraid. Tai startled and bumped into a tree, hearing one whisper clearly.

You're safe here. Stay.

Opening his eyes, he whirled around to see the fog had become more dense, and the trees continued to sway. He was winded, as though he'd been running, and called out in a voice unlike his own "Who's there?"

We're here, he heard - from all around him. *We've always been here.* Tai lunged behind trees, but whether he was searching anymore or hiding, he wasn't sure. Searching... what had he been searching for? His friends, maybe. Maybe the voices were his friends, playing a trick on him. James, and... and the other ones.

"Guys? Is that you?" Tai called out, but his voice only came out in a low, breathy tone.

We're here, the voice reassured, *we'll never leave you. Don't leave. Isn't it beautiful here?*

It really was beautiful, Tai thought, nodding and stepping out from behind another tree. He wandered forward in a daze. Colors melded together, all varying hues of greys and blues and browns. There was no trail to follow, so he shuffled between the trees, staring into the canopy of branches.

Fog rose from the ground to meet him, tasting his skin. It felt cool but not unpleasant, and smelled of the sea. The scent brought a flashing image - brilliant blue waters, glinting in the sunlight. His fingers flexed, searching for a vivid yellow board he'd forgotten about. Taking a deep breath and shaking his head, Tai stumbled.

The fog lifted, both from around him and within him, and he whipped his head back and forth, searching for... what *had* he been looking for? He closed his eyes and brought back to mind that scene of the beach. Clarity hit with the blunt end of reality, and he remembered Sonya, running away from him into the trees.

These trees - where the canopy created a permanent twilight, and whispers told people to stay. He broke into a slow jog, keeping the image of Sonya in his mind. In response, the fog thinned, allowing him to see farther. It felt like he jogged for hours... but that couldn't be. The island wasn't even that big, he reasoned. It was just the shadows playing tricks on him.

Her bright pink toenails were the first thing he saw, because he nearly ran into them face-first. Instinct had him jerking to the side to avoid a collision, stumbling into a tree as he stopped. Relief mingled with confusion as he caught his breath; Sonya, never the outdoorsy type, had run into the woods and climbed a tree?

With a half grin, he looked up - and saw that she wasn't on any branch. She hadn't climbed any of the trees. Instead, her body swayed back and forth, and her face had turned the color of the trees around them.

She was shades of blue and grey. Her shoulders slumped forward, and her head sat heavily to the side. Tai fell to his knees, unable to look away until he finally turned to retch at the base of the tree.

When he turned back to Sonya, he saw the rope she hung from had drawn her higher. Tears made tracks down his face as he knelt, willing her to move. He needed her to make a joke. To yell at him again; to do *anything*. Higher she rose, until he could barely make out her face.

It seemed worse somehow, that she was swaying. Death was supposed to mean not moving. His gaze drifted from her lifeless body into the treetops, where he could now make out others. What he had taken as swaying boughs were swaying bodies. Horror ran through him; a reckless child with scissors cutting him from the inside out.